W9-CZN-099

Scaredy Cat

For Judith Grant

Also by Joan Rankin

The Little Cat and the Greedy Old Woman
(A Margaret K. McElderry Book)

Margaret K. McElderry Books
An imprint of Simon & Schuster Children's Publishing Division
1230 Avenue of the Americas
New York, NY 10020

Copyright © 1996 by Joan Rankin

All rights reserved including the right of reproduction in whole or in part in any form.

First published in London by the Bodley Head Children's Books
First U.S. Edition 1996

Printed in Hong Kong

By arrangement with The Inkman, Cape Town, South Africa

10 9 8 7 6 5 4 3 2 1

Library of Congress Cataloging-in-Publication Data
Rankin, Joan.
Scaredy cat / [story and pictures by] Joan Rankin.—1st U.S. ed.
p.   cm.
"First published in London by the Bodley Head Children's Books"—T.p. verso.
Summary: A little kitten fearfully faces scary things such as a huge figure
on the wall, but when he encounters a tiny spider,
he discovers a bravery deep inside himself.
ISBN 0-689-80948-4
[1. Cats—Fiction. 2. Fear—Fiction.] I. Title.
PZ7.R16815Sh   1996
[E]—dc20
95-47597
CIP
AC

Scaredy Cat

Joan Rankin

MARGARET K. McELDERRY BOOKS

NEW HANOVER COUNTY
PUBLIC LIBRARY
201 CHESTNUT STREET
WILMINGTON, N C 28401

I don't like

Giants

but …

Mama Meow says
it's only Auntie B.

I am frightened of
Crocodiles
but…

Mama Meow says
they are only Auntie B.'s shoes.

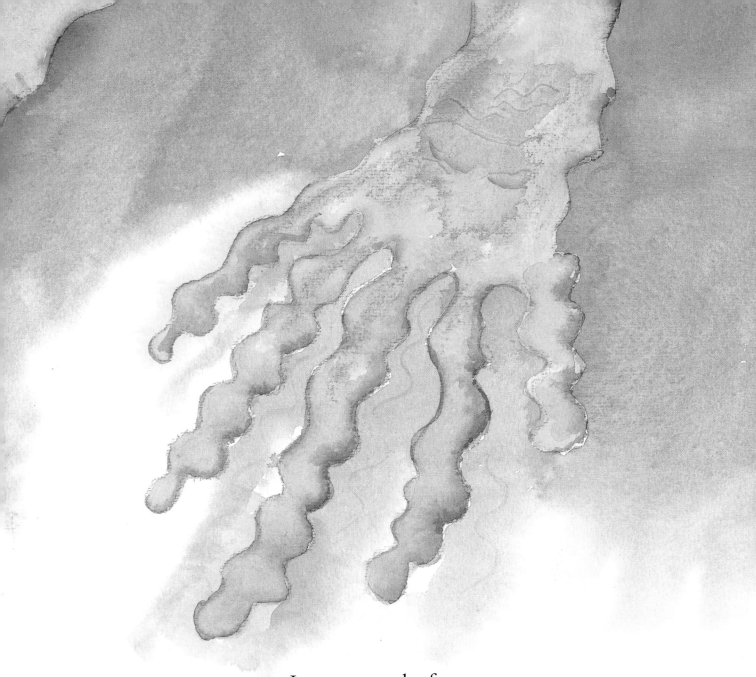

I am scared of

Wiggly
Thingamajigs

but…

Mama Meow says
they are only Auntie B.'s hands
wanting to cuddle me.

I am terrified of the

Screaming Sucking Monster

but…

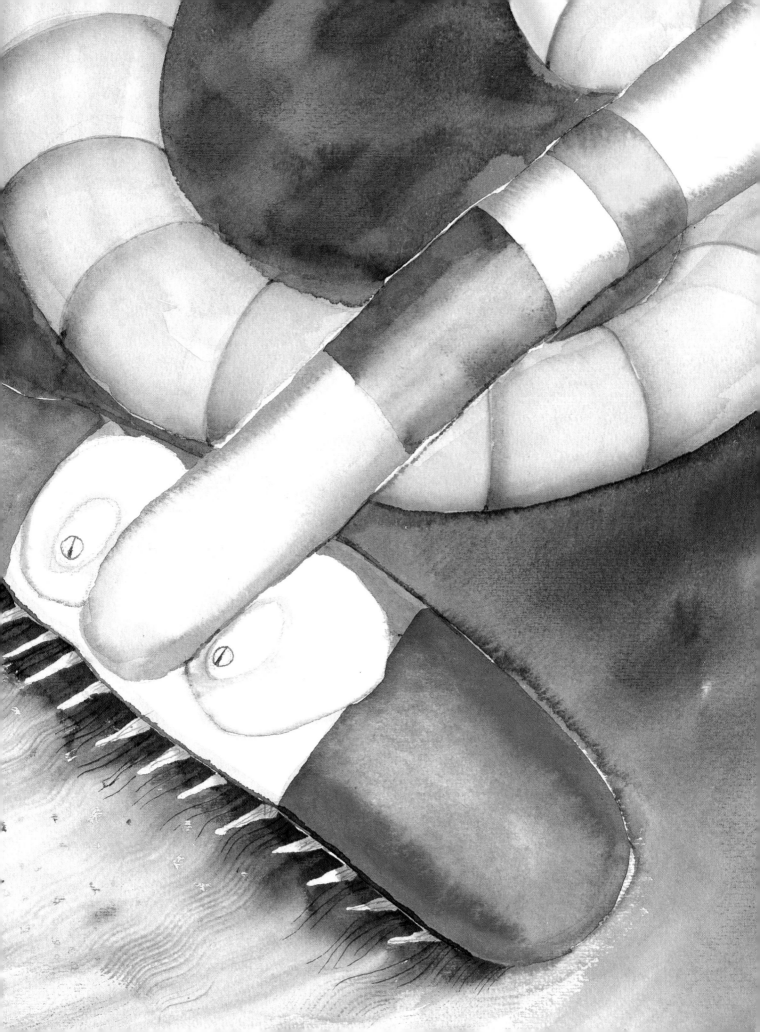

Mama Meow says
it is only Auntie B.'s vacuum cleaner
and Auntie B. won't let it
swallow me.

Ooooh!

A Dark
Hairy Forest!

Quick, quick!
I dash up onto Auntie B.'s lap
and hide in something warm
and woolly.

Auntie B. says
there's no need to worry,
it's only Scratchpooch.
But when *I* look out
all I see is…

an eensie-weensie spider,

looking straight at me.

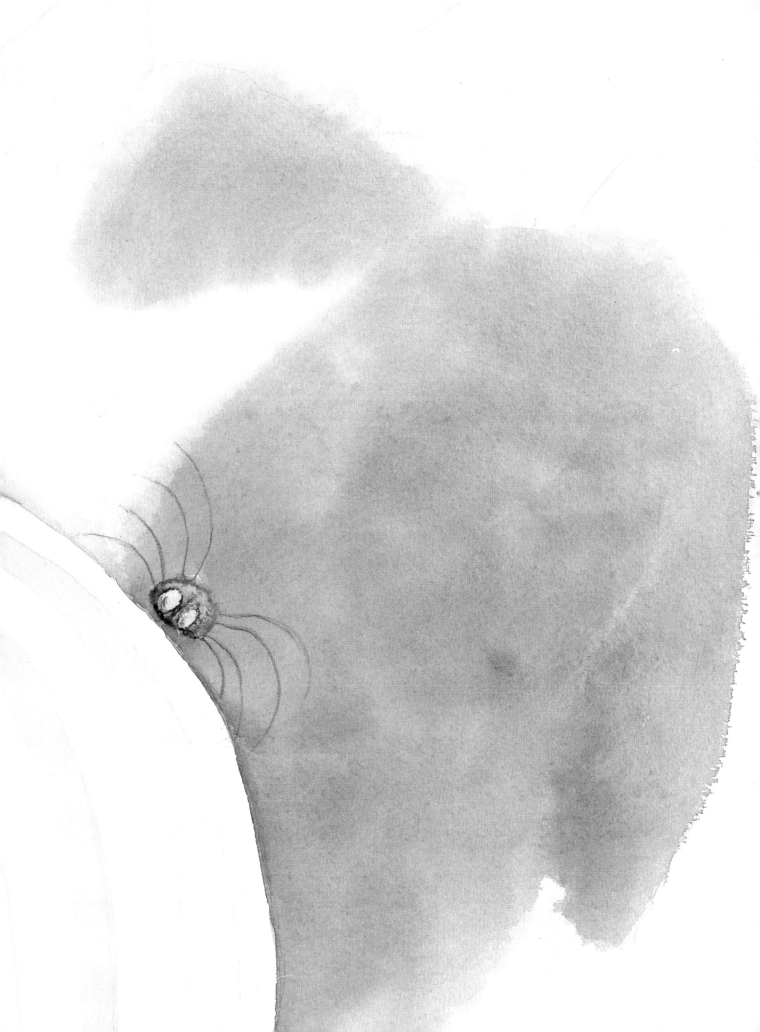

And if I stretch out my paw…

and fan out my claws…

I can

bonk

that eensie-weensie spider
on his head.

YEO

Kapow!

Just listen to him yell!

Mama Meow
says I'm her Tiger Cat
because I'm not scared of

Giants,
Crocodiles,
Wiggly
Thingamajigs,
Screaming Sucking
Monsters,
or A Dark Hairy
Forest.

And

WOW!....

are eensie-weensie spiders
scared of me!

Noted
7/31/00
SSD

NEW HANOVER COUNTY PUBLIC LIBRARY

11/96

NEW HANOVER COUNTY PUBLIC LIBRARY
201 Chestnut Street
Wilmington, N.C. 28401

GAYLORD S